May's CAKE

Written by Sydney Squires

Illustrated by Zannatul Zerin

- To Mom and Dad with love -

Challenge Words

ruin

bread

heard

flowers

brother

show

CHAPTER 1

May loved her family and wanted to help them.

One day, she cleaned all the dishes.

The next day,
she played with
her brother,
Matt, so that her
mom could rest.

Matt did not say
much, but he was so
cute and fun.

The day
after that,
she and
Mom
shopped for
food.

Then, she
helped Miss
Smith in the
yard.

Some days,
she helped
bake a yummy
treat for her
family.

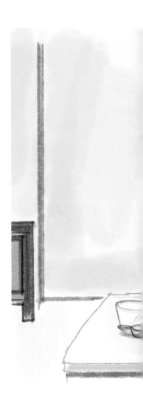

Other days, she helped Mom and Dad clean their home.

On Sundays, she helped Matt at church.

"We have to be good at church," she said.

Matt did not say much. He was too small. He just sat on her lap and smiled.

One day, Dad sat down with May.

"This week is a fun week," Dad said.

"This week is Mom's birthday," Dad said.

"Oh!" May was happy. "I want to make a gift for Mom!" She wanted to think of what she could do.

She could buy a dress that was blue with small flowers.

She could make drawings of Mom and put them on the walls.

She could make a home for the singing birds in the yard for Mom.

"Oh!" May told him.
"I will make a cake for
Mom."

"That is a good plan,"
Dad said. "You can
ask Uncle Ben to help
you in his bake shop!
Mom's birthday is in
three days."

"I will go and ask for
his help in three days,"
May said.

CHAPTER 2

May liked to think of what she wanted the cake to look like. The cake could be small, fat, and green.

The cake could be three feet tall!

"The cake could look like you, Matt," May said.

Matt was playing with his cars. He did not look up.

On Tuesday, May went to Uncle Ben's shop. The air smelled sweet and warm.

She saw all sorts of cakes—tall cakes, small cakes, red cakes, pink cakes!

Uncle Ben smiled.
"How are you, May?"

"Good!" May said.
"It is Mom's birthday.
I want to make her a

cake that is blue with small flowers on it. Then Mom will see how much I love her."

He took her to the back of the shop to make the cake. Then they mixed the cake.

Then they let
the cake bake.

While the cake was baking, they mixed the blue frosting.

"You have to wait until it cools so the frosting does not melt," Uncle Ben said when the cake was done. While May waited, she helped Uncle Ben.

She swept the floor.

She helped sell cakes.

She put fresh bread in the basket.

"The cake is cool now," Uncle Ben told her. He helped her frost the cake. It was blue and smooth.

"I love it!" May said. "Mom will love it, too!"

May was happy with her cake.

Her uncle smiled.
"Your mom will love
the cake." He put the
cake in a box.

"Take care, May," he
said to her.

"If you go too fast or if you fall, the cake will be ruined."

May nodded. "Thank you for your help," she said.

She held the box in both hands and left to go home.

CHAPTER 3

It was not a long walk, but May took her time. Uncle Ben had said to do so, and she did not want to ruin the cake.

The leaves were red and yellow. The air was crisp and cool.

The sky was blue, the same color as the cake.

May wanted to look at
the leaves and the sky
as she walked, but she
did not want to fall and
drop the cake.

She looked down and saw a big rock.

She walked around it.

There was a tree branch. She ducked under it.

"I will get this cake
home safely," May said.
She was happy. She
could not wait to show
Mom the cake.

Just then, she heard a cry. "Help! Help!"

May looked down at the box. She did not want to ruin her cake. But it is good to help

others. She ran to see if she could help.

"Help!" a girl called out. She was on a bike in the mud.

"I rode my bike into the mud, and now I cannot get out!"

May set her cake box down on the rock. "I can help." She took the

bike and the two girls
tugged. The bike came
out.

"Thank you so much
for your help!" the girl
said.

May went on her way.

"I hope I did not ruin my cake," she said. "Helping others is good. But I want to show Mom how much I love her!"

CHAPTER 4

May did not look at her cake until she got home. She looked in her box.

"Oh no!" she said.

The cake was not smooth. Some of the

frosting had fallen off.
It fell to one side.

"I ruined the cake!"
May shouted.

Dad came in. "May?
What is the matter?"

"I ruined the cake." May showed him the cake. "Now Mom will never see how much I love her."

May was so sad!

Dad gave May a big
hug.

"May, there are many ways to tell others that you love them."

May sniffed. "Really?"

"Really," Dad said. "It is okay that the cake fell down. You made a cake, and it is still a good cake that she will love."

May smiled.

"Mom will be home soon," Dad said. "She will love your cake. Here, let us set up for the party."

May mopped the floor.

Dad cleaned the dishes.

May picked flowers
and put them in a vase.

"There we go," Dad
said. "It is clean."

May nodded. She
could not wait for Mom
to come home.

CHAPTER 5

Just then, there was a *rap, rap, rap.*

"Who is here?" Dad asked.

May went to look. "Uncle Ben! And Mom!" She hugged them. "Happy birthday, Mom!"

"May has something to show you," Dad said.

May turned red. She did not want to show Mom her cake.

Then she told herself, "Mom knows I love her. I still made a cake, even if it is not the cake that I wanted."

She showed Mom the
blue cake.

"Uncle Ben
helped me make a
pretty cake for you.
I walked home,
but a girl called for
help! She was stuck

in the mud. I ran to
help her, and I ruined
your cake. Now it
looks like it may fall
down and some of
the frosting is gone."

Mom smiled. "Thank you for thinking of me and making this cake," she said.

"I am so glad that you ran to help that girl."

"Happy Birthday, Mom!" May said. "I love you!"